# SPLINTER TO THE FORE

Other Teenage Mutant Ninja Turtles® books available in Yearling Books:

*Teenage Mutant Ninja Turtles*®
    (a novelization of the movie) by B. B. Hiller
*Teenage Mutant Ninja Turtles,*® *The Secret of the Ooze*
    (a novelization of the movie) by B. B. Hiller
*Buried Treasure* by Dave Morris
*Sky High* by Dave Morris
*Red Herrings* by Dave Morris
*Six-Guns and Shurikens* by Dave Morris
*Dinosaur Farm* by Dave Morris

# TEENAGE MUTANT NINJA TURTLES®

# SPLINTER TO THE FORE

## DAVE MORRIS

*Illustrated by Phil Jacobs*

**A YEARLING BOOK**

Published by
Dell Publishing
a division of
Bantam Doubleday Dell Publishing Group, Inc.
666 Fifth Avenue
New York, New York 10103

This work was first published in Great Britain by Yearling Books,
Transworld Publishers Ltd.

ISBN: 0-440-40492-4

Printed in the United States of America

March 1991

10  9  8  7  6  5  4  3  2  1

OPM

# HEROES IN A HALF SHELL

Fourteen years ago, a group of four ordinary turtles that had dropped into the storm drains beneath New York were found by Splinter, a master of the skill of ninjutsu—the ancient Japanese art of stealth and espionage.

Then . . . a leakage of radioactive goo exposed Splinter and his pets to mutating chemicals. Splinter turned into a giant talking rat, while the turtles became the Teenage Mutant Ninja Turtles: his wacky, wisecracking, crime-fighting pupils.

With their human friend, April O'Neil, ace reporter on the Channel 6 TV News, the Turtles fight for what's right and foil the nefarious schemes of the Shredder—Splinter's evil renegade student.

Meet Leonardo, the coolly efficient, sword-swinging team leader. Meet Donatello, the expert when it comes to machines; his swishing quarterstaff lays out his foes like bowling pins. Meet Raphael, the prankster, whose wry humor sees the team through perilous situations while his twin daggers send enemies fleeing in panic. And meet Michaelangelo, who's a master of the whirling nunchakus and is prepared to use them on anyone who gets between him and a pizza!

Splinter just could not understand the Turtles sometimes.

Those were the times, like now, when their natural youthful excitement got in the way of their attention to study. Splinter had been spending most of the morning taking them through some advanced ninjitsu moves. But it is hard work training to be a ninja, especially for a bunch of high-spirited mutant teenagers. Michaelangelo's stomach rumbled every time he let his thoughts stray on to pizza—which was more and more frequently as the lesson went on. Raphael kept chewing a lump of gum and blowing bubbles that distracted him from the exercises he was supposed to be doing, and Donatello had taken to casting longing glances at his skateboard in the corner. Even the usually diligent Leonardo seemed fretful.

Splinter loved his pupils as if they were his own sons, and he made every effort to allow for their occasional impatience. As typical youngsters, they expected to master everything overnight. Splinter knew that becoming a good ninja required lots of practice and a constant striving to achieve complete unity between mind and body.

At last he gave a sigh. "Your spirits are distracted, my sons," he said. "Until you possess the right thinking, you can never advance in your mastery of ninjitsu."

Raphael spoke up. "Sorry, Master, but we've been cooped up down here for so long, we're beginning to feel like sardines in a can."

"That's odd," said Michaelangelo. "I feel like a pizza in a tray. Guess we could have sardines as a topping, though."

Splinter knew what Raphael meant. "I understand your feelings," he said. "It is hard to remain secluded away from the world, but that is the way of ninjitsu. If ever we show ourselves by day in the open, we must be sure to wear our disguises. The ninja's life is a life of secrecy, and the fewer people who know of our existence the better."

"We did come pretty close to being filmed by a camera crew during our last adventure," conceded Donatello.

"Worrywart," muttered Michaelangelo, who nursed a secret fantasy of being a TV star.

"Don's right, Mike," said Leonardo.

But he had an idea. "Couldn't we take an outing, Master? Jogging along the storm drains would be good exercise, and we'd still be keeping out of sight."

Splinter nodded. "Very well. Staying stuck between the four walls of the den cannot be good for you, I agree. Take an hour off to enjoy yourselves—but be back in an hour, and mind that no one sees you."

"Phew!" Raphael exclaimed as they were jogging along the sewer tunnels a few minutes later. "I'd forgotten what a stench there was down here in summer. Did anyone bring a clothespin?"

"Why, were you thinking of doing the laundry?" asked Michaelangelo.

"For my nose, dummy!" Raphael answered, giving his brother a good-natured slap across the head for being so dense.

"Gangway!" Donatello shouted. "Coming through, dudes!" He skidded past the others on his skateboard, showering them with water from the tunnel floor as he went by.

"*Water* revolting thing to do," said Raphael, taking off his bandana and wringing it dry. "Just *wet* till I get my hands on you, Don!"

"Yeah!" said Leonardo, spluttering. "I reckon we owe our bro' a ducking, huh, dudes?"

It was too much for Donatello to resist. Looking back with a wicked grin, he said, "You'll have to *catch* me first, you slowpokes." And with that he skated off along the tunnel.

"Yay!" the three of them cried, immediately giving chase. They were all eager for a bit of good horseplay after the serious training of the last few weeks. They sloshed along the tunnel without worrying how wet they got.

Suddenly Donatello pulled his skateboard to a halt. "Shush . . ." he said, but the others were on him in a second. Yelling happily, they dunked him under the water.

"Listen to me, you guys . . ." Donatello protested as he struggled out of their grip.

"It's a trick," said Raphael, unimpressed.

"Yeah, Don, you don't get off that lightly, you roadhog," said Michaelangelo.

"Tunnelhog," corrected Donatello. "But I really did hear something. Listen!"

"He's right," Leonardo said abruptly, silencing the others with a gesture. "There's someone up ahead."

Alerted now, the four Turtles advanced slowly to confront the intruder. Looming on the tunnel wall, they could now see a shadow cast by light from a grating. The muffled traffic sounds of the street filtered down from above.

"Careful, now," Leonardo whispered. "We don't want to be spotted. Remember what Splinter said."

Raphael glared at the shadow. Whoever it was, it was getting closer. And it was moving almost as silently as the Turtles themselves. "There's only one of them," he remarked softly.

"Don't underestimate the foe, Raph," said Donatello. It could have been Splinter himself talking. "Like Aesop said—only one, but a *lion*."

The mysterious figure came into view and instantly froze at the sight of four figures crouched in the shadows. Dressed all in black and wearing a mask, the figure reached for a tonfa club hanging at its belt.

"Jump him!" cried Leonardo.

The figure gave a grunt of surprise as the Turtles launched themselves out of the darkness into the light glinting down through the drain grating. "Wait . . ." a voice said, its accent obviously foreign. The tonfa was only half raised as Michaelangelo's fist slammed into the figure's jaw, scoring an instant knockout.

Leonardo reached past and pulled off the mask. "It's a woman!" He gasped.

The others crowded around for a look. "She's Japanese," said Donatello.

"Mike, you dope," Raphael grumbled, "she wasn't going to fight us. Didn't you hear her say *wait?*"

Michaelangelo spread his hands. "Oh, that's it, blame me. I just did what Leo told me. Hey, look at that symbol on her headband. Isn't that the mark of The Foot?" He pointed to a scarlet dragon insignia.

Donatello took a closer look and shook his head. "No—Shredder's Foot Soldiers wear the symbol of a clawed dragon with open wings. This dragon is more serpentine, and it doesn't have any wings."

"Guess I don't even get three out of ten for identification," admitted Michaelangelo, "but I'm sure she's coming round."

The woman gave a groan and sat up, rubbing a bump where she had hit her head falling. "You must be the Teenage

Mutant Ninja Turtles," she said. "Tell me, are you always so hostile to visitors?"

"It pays to be jumpy, with the kind of visitors you get down here," explained Raphael. "We don't exactly get the mailman calling to tell us we've won the New York lottery, y'know?"

Leonardo had other things on his mind. "Would you mind telling us who you are? And how you know about us?"

The woman got to her feet and hooked the tonfa club back on her belt. "I'm Murazumi Mieko. I'm a ninja, like you," she said. "And although your existence isn't common knowledge, word does get around among the world's ninja community when somebody keeps giving a big cheese like Oroku Saki a hard time."

"Oroku Saki! The Shredder!" The Turtles were immediately on their guard again.

"So you *are* on his side!" exclaimed Michaelangelo. "I knew it!"

"There you go again," said Mieko. "Why don't you wait to hear the whole story before you start getting steamed up?"

"She's right, guys," said Raphael. "Why don't we listen to the full story, *then* get steamed up?"

"Okay, we will," Leonardo told Mieko. "Maybe you'd better come back with us and have a word with our sensei, Master Splinter. But don't try any tricks."

"I don't know any tricks," Mieko said with a smile. "But if any of you do, maybe you could just make this lump on my head disappear."

As they were approaching the secret den where the Turtles lived, Leonardo asked Mieko what she was doing in the storm drains.

"Looking for you, obviously," she said.

"How did you know we lived down here?" Michaelangelo asked.

"I didn't—not for certain. But the

drains are damp and secret—and they provide an easy way of getting around town without being seen. What better hideout could there be for a group of turtle ninjas?"

"You were lucky that we ran into you," Raphael said.

"I'm still not sure about that." Mieko was fingering the bump on her head.

"What Raph means," said Donatello, "is that you never would have found our den just wandering around." He turned down yet another sewer—then pulled open a door.

As she stepped through, Mieko realized that Donatello was right—there was no way anybody could stumble on to the Turtles' lair by accident, for it was situated in the midst of a confusing maze of tunnels.

As they entered the den, Splinter was sitting cross-legged in his favorite armchair, deep in meditation. If he was startled to see his pupils bringing back a visitor, it hardly showed in more than a flicker of his bristly eyebrows.

"Master," began Leonardo. "This is Mieko. She was prowling around the sewers looking for this place."

"I resent the world 'prowling,' " said Mieko, staring in amazement at the mutant rat sitting in front of her. "But yes, I was looking for your pupils—only they found me first."

Splinter saw her wince as she touched her bruise. "Ah, my sons," he said sorrowfully, "how many times have I told you that violence is to be used only when all else fails? It is the first action of the ignorant."

"That's okay, then, Master," Raphael said with a smile, "because it was Mike who slugged her—and he's ignorant, all right."

Michaelangelo took a moment to realize he was being insulted. Before he could reply, Splinter raised his hands for them all to be silent. "Let us hear our guest's tale from her own lips," he suggested. "Won't you sit down?" he continued, looking toward their visitor. Mieko settled on the sofa in front of him. "Mieko . . . Mieko?" he repeated thoughtfully. "Why is that name familiar?"

"I don't know any reason why it should be," admitted Mieko. "I've never met any rats before. Nor turtles, for that matter. When the rumor got around of a group of mutant ninja operating here in America—and quashing the Shredder's schemes time and again—my master looked into the few firsthand reports. He says that your fighting style is very similar to that used by our group. And that led him to think that your master must once have belonged to his own former clan."

"Which was . . . ?" asked Splinter.

"The Foot Clan," replied Mieko.

"I knew it! I told you!" Michaelangelo burst out. "She's with Shredder's gang!"

"Michaelangelo!" Splinter reprimanded. "You are being very rude to our guest. She said that her master *formerly* belonged to The Foot—as did I, in fact, many years ago. It was not always the evil organization that it has become under the Shredder's villainous leadership. Once The Foot was an honorable clan."

"Excuse me," said Mieko, leaning forward and staring at Splinter. "You say you were once a member of The Foot? I know things were different in the old days, but don't tell me they were in the habit of admitting rodents then."

"The same radioactive substance that gave my pupils their mutant form also changed me. Now I am half rat, but long ago I was a human called Hamato Yoshi."

Mieko's mouth fell open. "Master Yoshi? I remember you."

"And I remember you now, Murazumi Mieko," Splinter said with a warm smile as he cast his mind back. "You were just a child when you first came to my dojo. It was not long after that Shredder turned the clan into an army of criminals."

Mieko fell to her knees and bowed.

"Forgive me for not recognizing you at once, Master Yoshi," she said.

"Sheesh, she's sure changed her tune," Raphael said under his breath. "She's not interested in *us* anymore."

Mieko did not hear. She was still too astonished at seeing the transformation that had come over her old tutor. After a moment she continued with her story. "Once Oroku Saki took over The Foot, many of us refused to go along with his evil ways. We left and joined a splinter group—"

"I'm sure that wasn't meant to be a pun," interrupted Raphael.

Mieko glanced at him impatiently. "A splinter group called The Little Toe. We maintain the noble traditions of the clan's founders, working only to protect others and do good."

"Well, our little 'Splinter' group has traditions of its own, Mieko," said Splinter, "and one of those is a rather unusual, er, delicacy called pizza. Will you join us for a slice while you tell us why you've come?"

"Excellent!" cried Donatello.

"Bodacious!" exclaimed Raphael.

"Triumphant!" said Leonardo.

"Deep-dish hot chili-pepper special with no anchovies!" Michaelangelo called out.

As they sat down to eat, Mieko told them why she had gone to such pains to find them. "Our clan has been employed by the Kito Leisure Corporation, which is building a hotel and pleasure park in upstate New York. When it's finished there'll be sports fields, a wildlife area, hotels, swimming pools, a golf course, a theme park—you name it, they'll have it."

"Just like Disneyland," breathed Michaelangelo, "but here in New York State! Can we go, Master?"

"Michaelangelo," said Splinter, "it isn't even built yet."

"It may never be," said Mieko, struggling to pick up a slice of pizza with her chopsticks. "The whole project has been dogged by trouble since day one. It started with minor things like digging equipment going wrong, then newly laid foundations gave way on the hotel site. Since then it's gotten worse and worse, and what seemed at first to be bad luck is now looking more and more like sabotage. The Kito Corp engaged us to find out what's happening and get the people responsible to stop it, but so far we've drawn a complete blank."

"Hmm," Splinter looked at his own meal—a sushi tray rather than pizza—and rubbed his nose. "Very vexing. If you cannot complete your assignment, then the clan will be disgraced still further than it has been by Saki's misdeeds, and the reputation handed down to us by our ancestors becomes dishonored."

"How fortunate that my search for the Turtles led me to you, Yoshi-sama," said Mieko. "As a former member of our clan, you can understand the nature of our plight."

"I prefer the name Splinter now—but yes, you are right, Mieko. To retain one's honor is vital. My pupils and I also hold with the original, good intentions of the ninja art. We will help."

"I just had a nasty thought, dudes," Donatello said as they were washing the dishes later. "Who's got more reason than anyone to try to disgrace the break-away ninja group?"

"Shredder," said Raphael. "He's mean enough, all right."

"Uh . . . Shredder's the least of our worries right now, guys."

"What do you mean, Mike?" Leonardo asked seriously. "What's wrong?"

"We've run out of dishwashing detergent," replied Michaelangelo, holding up the empty bottle. "And we've still got *yesterday's* dishes to do as well."

Much to the Turtles' delight, it turned out that Mieko had made her journey down to the city by light plane. It promised to be an exciting journey back to the development site upstate. They reached the airfield around dawn, and Splinter and his pupils used the cover of the early-morning twilight to creep aboard the aircraft unseen. Meanwhile, Mieko—now dressed in designer overalls instead of her ninja gear—went to the flight control building to log out.

"We've brought our operation up to date a bit in the last few years," she explained when she got back. "Skulking about everywhere in masks and black pajama suits is a little too conspicuous in the modern world, you know?"

"Tell us about it," said Leonardo, nodding his head. "Shredder's thugs always stick out like sore thumbs."

"There could be a joke in that," said Michaelangelo. "Y'know: 'When is a Foot like a thumb?' . . ."

"Believe me, Mike," said Leonardo, "if I'd thought the crack was worth making, I'd have made it myself."

"Will the trip take long?" Raphael asked with a groan as Mieko taxied the plane to the start of the runway. "When I was talking about sardines yesterday, I didn't know the half of it." He shifted uncomfortably, trying in vain to find some leg room.

"This is a Cessna 182, Raph," Donatello said authoritatively. "It's only supposed to carry a couple of passengers."

"Actually it's a Turbo Skyline RG II," said Mieko. "Like the 182 but with some nifty extras. The turbo-charged engine should cope quite nicely with the extra payload."

"Hah-hah, Mr. Know-it-all," Raphael jeered at Donatello. It cheered him up a little to find that his brother was not always right about everything.

Having run through the preflight check, Mieko opened up the throttle. The plane began to accelerate down the runway.

Splinter, who was perched beside her on the passenger seat, glanced at the airspeed indicator and then looked out of the window. "Hmm," he remarked with only a slight quaver in his tranquil voice, "this is somewhat faster than the Turtle Blimp."

A grove of trees lay less than a hundred yards ahead. Michaelangelo stared over the back of the seat, gaping in horror, then put his fingers over his eyes. "We're gonna crash! We're gonna crash!" he yelled, half pulling his head back into his shell.

"Relax, Mike," Donatello said reassuringly after a few moments. "We're airborne."

"We are?" Michaelangelo took a peek. "We *are!*" He stared out of the window as the fields surrounding the airstrip dropped away beneath them. "Wow, this is great!"

"It is a bit noisier than the Blimp, though!" said Leonardo, almost having to shout over the roar of the engine.

It was a warm day with very few clouds, and they were soon cruising north with the ground whipping past thousands of feet below. In less than an hour Mieko announced that she was beginning the descent. "Kito Corp has established a private airstrip on the land they've bought," she explained. "There won't be many people around, but I suggest you get into your disguises, just in case."

"It's a bit hot for this kind of stuff today," Raphael complained as he pulled on a hat and trench coat.

"So, we could hardly disguise ourselves with shorts and sunglasses, could we, Raph?" Leonardo replied. "Also, you've just put your arm into the sleeve of my trench coat."

Amid grumbles and occasional thumps as they scrambled about in the cramped space, the Turtles struggled to disentangle themselves and put their disguises on. Splinter, meanwhile, had donned a deerstalker hat and long Inverness cape, and looked somewhat like Sherlock Holmes.

Suddenly Mieko spoke up, a tone of rising panic in her voice.

"Master Splinter!" she exclaimed. "The landing gear indicator hasn't come on."

Splinter was a master of ninjitsu, but

he knew very little about machines. "What does that mean?"

Mieko's lips were pressed together in worry. She pulled back on the stick to reduce their rate of descent. "It means the undercarriage hasn't lowered properly. If we land without it the plane would be ripped apart on impact. Like opening a can."

"That sardine analogy is getting tedious," said Raphael.

"Or it might just mean a bulb's gone on the control panel . . . ?" suggested Michaelangelo.

Mieko swallowed nervously. "The only way to find that out is to land!"

"Well, we can't stay up here all day," said Leonardo. "And I don't think the emergency repairman will be dropping by at three thousand feet up."

"So, why not join the MKAC?" said Donatello, rummaging inside his knapsack. After a moment he held up a fistful of screwdrivers and other tools.

"What does MKAC stand for?" asked Raphael.

"The Mr. Know-it-all Airplane Club, of course," said Donatello with a grin. He began to open the door.

"Oh, no!" protested Raphael. "Don— I'm sorry I said that earlier, but please . . . don't go clambering around outside without a parachute, huh? If you fall from this height, there won't be enough left of you to fill a pizza tray!"

"You'd be teen, green, and smithereens," agreed Michaelangelo, nodding vigorously.

Leonardo thought for a moment. "I don't think we have a choice. If Don doesn't fix the landing gear then we've all had it. But just climbing out is no good—at this speed, there's a good chance of the wind blowing you off the side. I have a plan to make it a bit safer."

After hastily consulting with Splinter and the others, Leonardo explained his idea and they set about putting it into practice. Splinter and Leonardo braced themselves and, taking hold of Raphael's and Michaelangelo's legs, lowered them out of either side of the plane. Raphael and Michaelangelo then dangled down headfirst and stretched one of the trench coats between their hands so that it hung under the plane like a hammock. As Mieko reduced air speed as much as she could, Donatello scrambled down and tied himself into the makeshift hammock so that he had both hands free to work on the jammed undercarriage.

"We ought to form an aerial stunt team," said Leonardo, gritting his teeth with the strain.

"I think . . . that's what we just have done . . . Leonardo," Splinter said with a grunt. The venerable rat was not as strong as his young pupils, but his iron-hard determination meant that he would be pulled out rather than release his grip on Michaelangelo's feet.

Donatello, meanwhile, was working feverishly at the landing gear. Swaying sickeningly in the gusting wind, he prod-

ded around the mechanism until he found the source of the trouble: a loose wire. The current tingled in his fingers as he twisted it back into place, but fortunately the voltage was not high enough to hurt him.

"I'm glad we didn't take the train," he yelled to Raphael. "I'd have been fried to a cinder trying a stunt like this on the railroad."

Raphael shook his head. He could not hear his brother over the noise of the wind and the engine. Suddenly his eyes widened in alarm. Donatello looked up to see the undercarriage unfolding toward him. Mieko had forgotten to turn off the switch, and now that Donatello had fixed the problem, the wheels were lowering as they were supposed to. The only trouble was, he was still in the way!

There were only moments before the force of the lowering wheels pushed him out of his brothers' grip. Donatello had to act fast. After grabbing Raphael's wrists, he kicked the bottom end of the hammock out of Michaelangelo's hands and swung right around in a backflip, swaying out from the plane until he could grab a handhold on the wing. He saw Leonardo's face at the open door, contorted with effort. Even Leonardo, strong as he was, could not hold the weight of both Raphael and Donatello for very long.

Fortunately he did not have to. Splinter had reacted as soon as he felt the strain lessen on his side, helping Michaelangelo back aboard so that all three could combine their efforts to haul Raphael and Donatello inside.

"Bogus!" exclaimed Michaelangelo, panting, when they were all safe and the doors were closed again. "I'll never complain about the Blimp ever again. Give me a more leisurely ride anytime!"

"Believe me," said Mieko, "landings aren't usually that hair-raising."

"Who said anything about hair?" replied Raphael, running a hand across his smooth scalp. "It's my breakfast that was coming up. Or was it going down? It's hard to tell which way is which when you're dangling around out there."

"Hold on to your seats," warned Mieko. A series of vibrating bumps told them they had touched down. "Sorry about the rough landing," she said as she taxied to a hangar. "I think my nerves are a bit frayed."

"Just like the loose wire I found," said Donatello. "And I'll tell you something else. It had been disconnected, but the contact had still been made for a while by sparking across the gap—that's why we were able to raise the undercarriage after leaving New York. It must have been doing that for some time because the insulation had actually been slightly blackened by continuous sparking."

"So? What are you saying, Don—in words of one syllable, please?" asked Leonardo.

"What I'm saying is, the landing gear was probably tampered with before

Mieko even left for New York City. Some-one here on the Kito Corp site didn't want her to live long enough to contact us!"

It wasn't long before Mieko was taking
Splinter and his pupils on a tour of the
perimeter wire fence around the con-
struction site.

"Wow!" said Michaelangelo, sniffing
the air. "Get a lungful of this fresh rural
atmosphere, guys—what a change from
the sewers! Don't you all just love the
unspoiled countryside?"

"Hmph," grumbled Raphael. "How long do you suppose it will stay unspoiled once they've built a few hotels here?"

Mieko stopped by the fence and waited with arms folded until she had their attention.

"This wire was put up to stop wild animals from wandering on to the site and getting hurt," she explained. "The Kito Corporation wasn't expecting intruders when it started work here."

"The fence doesn't seem to have been tampered with at any point," observed Splinter. "Any normal intruder would have had to cut his way through, surely."

"He could have climbed over?" Michaelangelo asked.

Splinter nodded. "In that case, we should find a point where the wire mesh is bent out of shape. It hardly looks sturdy enough to support a full-grown man's weight."

The others looked along the perimeter fence and groaned. "But, Master, there must be *miles* of fencing to look at," protested Raphael.

"All the more reason to get cracking!" said Splinter, striding off purposefully with one hand holding on to his hat to keep it from blowing off.

"Oh, boy, we've got our work cut out for us, dudes," said Leonardo.

"But we can save time if we split up. Mike, you and Don go with Mieko and check in that direction. Raph and I will help Splinter."

"But what are we looking for, Leo?" asked Michaelangelo.

"Anything. Wire bent out of shape, footprints, a torn scrap of clothing . . . Anything!"

Eventually it was Splinter's sharp eyesight that found the clue they were searching for. High up on the perimeter wire, he spotted something fluttering in the warm midday breeze. After calling the others together, he got Donatello to knock it down using the tip of his bo staff.

It turned out to be a tuft of reddish-brown fur.

"It's just a bit of fox fur, Master," said Michaelangelo, never slow to venture a hasty opinion.

"Michaelangelo," Splinter said patiently. "Look at the fence. What can you tell me about it?"

Michaelangelo stared at it and scratched his head. "Uh . . . well . . . it's made of wire, Master."

Splinter sighed. "Yes. Anything else? How high is it, for instance?"

"About twelve feet," estimated Michaelangelo. He pondered this for a moment. ". . . Oh, yeah, too high for a fox, I guess."

"The wire isn't bent at all," said Donatello, who had been making a closer inspection. "Whoever it was didn't climb over."

"Maybe he jumped," said Raphael.

"Pole-vaulted, more like" was Leonardo's opinion. He scrambled over the fence and took a look at the ground on

the other side. "There's no sign of a pole having been used, though," he called back. "It would certainly have left a mark in the grass here."

Splinter nodded sagely. "Let us review the facts. An intruder entered at this point, leaving a tuft of fox fur on the top of the wire fence. Since he neither climbed nor vaulted over, he must have crossed the fence in a straight jump. . . ."

"Twelve feet!" Leonardo exclaimed, climbing back to rejoin the others. "This intruder's in the wrong line of business; he ought to enter the Olympic games."

Mieko was looking very troubled. "This all seems disturbingly familiar. It reminds me of legends from when I was a kid. Master Splinter, you know the old folktales about *kitsune*: Thousand-Year Fox Spirits."

"Fox Spirits?" said Raphael. "What're they?"

"Kind of like Japanese genies," explained Mieko. "They look like foxes most of the time, but they can change their shape to look like anything they want. They have magical powers, and in fact many ninja believe that the original skills of ninjitsu were taught to mankind by the Fox Spirits."

"Wow!" said Michaelangelo. "And we're going to get to meet one."

"That could be a worrying thought," said Mieko. "The Fox Spirits are said to be sometimes benevolent, but just as often they can be hostile. If this is a Fox Spirit, and if it has a reason to want the leisure park project sabotaged, we may have bitten off more than we can chew."

"Not in Mike's case," said Raphael. "He never bites off so much that he can't manage to chew it."

"Yeah, he's a *snapper* turtle," said Leonardo.

"I'm not sure Mike is a turtle," said Donatello. "I sometimes think he's just a mutant waste disposal unit!"

"Aw, cut it out, you guys," Michaelangelo said. "What about it, Master—could this be the work of a Fox Spirit?"

Splinter stroked his jaw thoughtfully. "Hmm . . . I doubt it, my sons. There are too many 'ifs.' Even if Fox Spirits truly *did* exist, why should one leave its home in Japan and come all the way to the east coast of America?"

"Why not, Master?" Raphael asked. "You did."

"Moreover," continued Splinter, ignoring him, "how would a Fox Spirit know how to tamper with a plane?"

Mieko remained unconvinced by Splinter's skepticism. "I think I'm going to try getting hold of some dried fish," she said. "According to legend, Fox Spirits are very partial to dried fish, and I might be able to bait a trap with some."

Splinter shrugged. "I have nothing against you pursuing that line of investigation, Mieko. All the same, I suspect that there is a more logical explanation for what has been going on. My pupils and I will lie in wait tonight to see if the mysterious intruder comes back."

"A night under the stars," Raphael

muttered to his brothers as they walked back. "Just great! I'd rather be back in the den watching TV."

"Here's your chance to get a scout badge, Raph," joked Leonardo.

"I'll bring the marshmallows if you bring the root beer."

A few hours after sunset, the Turtles and
their master took up positions to await
the saboteur. The place they chose was
the golf course, because work had just
been completed there during the day. It
was due to open in a week's time, with a
major televised golf championship to
mark the occasion. As Splinter said, "If
the intruder wants to do some damage,

this is the most likely point for him to strike."

After concealing themselves in a bush under some trees, they waited until the moon set. It was now some time after midnight. In the distance an owl hooted.

Something had been bothering Michaelangelo for several hours. At last he could contain his curiosity no longer. "Master," he asked, "why do they call the level patch of grass around the hole the 'green'? The whole golf course is green, isn't it?"

"That lake there isn't," Donatello pointed out.

"Nor those big sandpits," said Leonardo. "It's a bit silly leaving those all over the course, isn't it? What if someone knocked his ball in there by accident?"

"They're called sand traps," said Splinter, who often watched golf coverage on late-night TV when the Turtles were asleep. "The whole purpose of the game is to get your ball into the little hole on the green while avoiding those obstacles. Now, be quiet, all of you—we don't want to scare the saboteur away."

- "I'm not sure he's coming at all," grumbled Raphael. "And my foot's gone to sleep, crouching here all this time." He twisted into a more comfortable position.

"What're you griping about, Raph?" said Leonardo. "At least it's a dry night. Imagine if we'd had to do this in midwinter."

"I'd rather not—" began Raphael. "Hey! Look over there!"

They peered out of the bushes to see a figure gliding across the golf course. As expert ninja they all had excellent night vision, but even so the figure was only just visible in the starlight. He was visiting each hole in turn, and seemed to be pouring something into each one from a canister he was carrying.

"What's he up to?" whispered Donatello. "I can't make out what that stuff is from here."

"I'll tell you what—I don't think he's

watering the flowers," Leonardo said. "Shall we jump him, Master?"

Splinter whispered, "I cautioned you only yesterday about using violence before you find out the full story. We shall follow him back to his lair. He may have accomplices, after all."

As the intruder finished his task and made off, the Turtles slipped out of the bushes and stealthily gave chase. As they passed one of the holes, Donatello checked it out and signaled to Splinter. "He's filled them with quick-dying cement. That would certainly have messed up the golf championship."

"Hey, let's not lose sight of that saboteur!"

As the intruder approached the perimeter fence, they were able to get closer and have a better look at him. What they saw was quite startling. Instead of a human, he was a short, lithe figure covered in fur. He was wearing a sort of harness made of metal links on which he had slung various bits and pieces—including something that looked very like a gun. And, most amazing of all, he had a tail.

"How's he going to get over the wire?" Leonardo whispered to the others.

The next moment, he got his answer. The bizarre figure stepped up toward the fence and suddenly took an extraordinary leap that carried him right over!

"That's some feat." Donatello whistled softly in admiration.

"That's *twelve* feet, to be precise," said Michaelangelo. "Hey, dudes, we mustn't let him get away."

After swiftly climbing over the fence, they stalked after the intruder. It was the most difficult task of shadowing they had ever had to do, and it took everything they had learned of the ancient art of invisibility. Every so often the intruder would stop and sniff the air, as if warned by a sixth sense that someone was following him. Once or twice he looked back and the Turtles had to take cover in the undergrowth quickly and noiselessly to avoid being spotted.

The pursuit led them for fifteen minutes into the forested hills north of the park site. Then, finally, their quarry reached his destination: a concealed tunnel into a mossy bank under the spreading limbs of a huge old oak.

Splinter drew his pupils to a halt and took stock of the situation. "We must proceed with caution," he told them. "You have already realized that our foe is alert and skillful. We must be no less so."

"Master," said Michaelangelo, speaking the question that was in all their minds, "*is* he a Fox Spirit? He looked an awful lot like one, and Mieko said that Fox Spirits were the ones who invented ninjitsu in the first place."

"Yeah," Raphael agreed. "Taking on a dude like that with ninjitsu would be like teaching our grandmother to suck eggs."

Leonardo glowered at them. "Our grandmother *laid* eggs, dummy—she didn't suck 'em!" He sounded confident to bolster up their spirits, but his whispered aside to Splinter was less assured: "What do you think, Master?"

"Our foe is good," conceded Splinter, his voice calmly authoritative. "That much I could tell by watching him try to shake off our pursuit. But nonetheless we managed to track him here, and our combined efforts will certainly prevail no matter how powerful he may be."

The Turtles began to move closer to the tunnel where they had seen the strange figure disappear. No light came from inside. With Leonardo leading the way, they groped along in darkness. Their previous uncertainty had been dispelled by Splinter's pep talk. Now they were quietly determined, weapons gripped confidently in their hands.

Donatello, however, still had doubts. "What about his magic?" he asked Splinter.

"Donatello, I am sure of one thing: This is no mythical werefox that we are up against. Such a creature could have taken any shape to fool us or throw us off his trail. Rest assured, our adversary's powers are purely natural."

"Quite correct," said a voice, "although not natural to *this* world."

They all whirled, for the voice had come from behind them. Somehow their adversary had lured them into a trap.

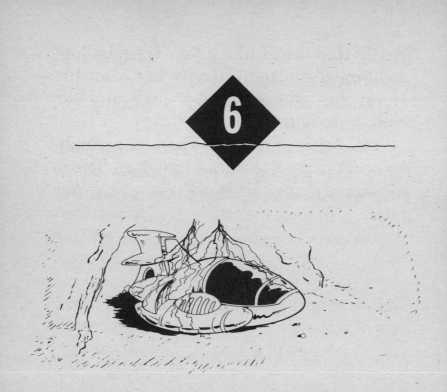

## 6

A flashlight snapped on, and they saw how the saboteur had managed to get around behind them. He was emerging from a concealed alcove in the side of the tunnel. He had been waiting there until they passed, ready to step out of hiding once he had them deep in his lair.

At close quarters, in the glare of the light, they could see that he was not really that much like a fox. True, he had red-brown fur and a bushy tail—but his snout was shorter than a fox's and his ears more batlike.

Shielding his eyes from the flashlight, Splinter took a step forward before he saw the gun in the saboteur's other hand. "Who are you?" he asked in an unconcerned tone. He wanted to buy time and calm the situation down. The Turtles were hotheaded enough to try jumping the stranger, and Splinter did not want one of them getting shot in the process.

"I am Karu," said the stranger, speaking into a microphone gadget attached to his harness that apparently translated his words. "As perhaps you are starting to guess, I am not from this planet. I am an interstellar traveler from a planet around the star you call Sirius."

"You cannot be *sirius*," said Raphael.

"You doubt the truth of what I say?" said Karu. "Look, Earthlings." He directed his flashlight past them along the tunnel.

*"Earthlings,"* said Donatello. "Now, that's not a phrase you hear much these days outside of bad 1950s films."

All the same, he turned with the others to look where Karu was pointing the beam. It illuminated the metallic outlines of a vehicle rather like a space capsule, nestling at the end of the tunnel. Even more remarkably, the roots of the oak tree they had seen above were growing right around the spaceship.

"You must've been on Earth a heck of a long time, dude," said Michaelangelo. "It looks like you're putting down roots."

"My species is very long-lived," conceded Karu. "I have been on your planet for hundreds of years. My people are renowned throughout the galaxy for their love of hunting, you see. We travel many light-years to find planets where the game is good. Earth has been excellent for this purpose, and my hunts here have been most enjoyable. It is one of the few unspoiled planets in this arm of the galaxy. Or it has been up until now. I doubt if it will last another hundred years, what with clearing all the woodland for building work and what-have-you."

"I tend to agree that too much of the world's natural beauty is being spoiled," said Splinter. "All the same, you cannot go around sabotaging development work just because it threatens to spoil your fun."

"Yeah, buster," said Michaelangelo, moving up beside his master. "I'd say you're a real undesirable alien!"

"Preposterous!" Karu snapped into his translator. "I do as I please. I was aware of your efforts to follow me, and I lured you back here so that I could trap you. Now, as you see, I hold the gun while you have only your little sticks and knives. So how do you propose to stop me?"

"Donatello," Splinter said in answer to the alien's tirade, "will you illuminate this fellow, please?"

Their words were likewise being translated back into Karu's language by his portable computer, so it took a fraction of a second for him to catch the meaning in what Splinter had just said. Before he could react, Donatello had flicked on his pencil flashlight and shone it straight into the alien's sensitive eyes.

"Ahhh!" shrieked Karu, throwing his hand up to shield his eyes. As he staggered back, dazzled, Splinter lunged forward to grapple with him.

But Karu recovered from the surprise faster than any of them had anticipated. As Splinter seized the hand holding the gun and forced it up, Karu squeezed the trigger. A blast of searing laser light shot over Splinter's head, singeing his fur, and stabbed into the tunnel roof. Amid a deafening rumble, dislodged earth and rocks showered down around them.

Still holding on to Karu, Splinter forced him back to the mouth of the tunnel. Suddenly they were clear of the falling debris and out in the fresh night air. As they both coughed the dust out of their lungs, Splinter looked back along

the tunnel and a sickening feeling closed around the pit of his stomach. The ray gun had caused a cave-in that completely blocked the tunnel. The Turtles were buried alive!

Splinter would have started to clear the rubble with his bare hands, but Karu gave him no chance for that. After leveling his ray gun, the alien fired at point-blank range. Anyone else would have been fried in his shoes—but Splinter did not wear shoes, and in any case he was too fast and wily to let himself get tagged by a laser beam. He executed a swift series of ninja moves to evade Karu's repeated shots and disappeared into a clump of bushes.

Karu stopped firing. Splinter had expected only a moment's respite, as the ray gun could obviously burn away the undergrowth quite quickly. It seemed that Karu was reluctant to risk a forest fire—or perhaps his gun carried only a limited charge.

There was silence, then the alien's translated and synthesized voice rang out. "Show yourself, Earth creature. If you come out of hiding right now, I will spare your life."

"No, Karu," Splinter called back. "Your words fall on deaf ears." He moved easily to one side to avoid the ray blast that Karu unleashed in the direction of his voice. *Good,* Splinter thought. *If that gun does have charges, I may be able to get him to waste them.*

He peered out of the foliage. Karu was unhooking another device from his harness and swinging it to and fro. Splinter guessed that it was some kind of infrared tracker. He glanced at the caved-in tunnel, then back down out of the woods toward the park site. Assuming the Turtles were still alive (and Splinter did not dare to think otherwise), they would even now be trying to dig their way out. If Karu was still here when they broke through the rockfall, he could pick them off like fish in a barrel. Splinter had to entice him away somehow. But how?

Then he remembered. Every foe is the key to his own defeat, and Karu had given Splinter the clue to his weakness. Using ventriloquism to throw his voice, Splinter cried out: "You underestimate your quarry, Karu. I doubt if you can hunt me."

A tree nearby erupted into flame from Karu's laser beam. Splinter threw his voice in the other direction: "Those high-tech toys of yours have made you weak, Karu. You no longer seem able even to shoot straight!"

Another blast all but vaporized a

shrub yards to Splinter's left. Well, he certainly had the alien's full attention now. With a taunting cry, he slipped silently down the hillside.

Karu came hot on his heels, firing laser shots whenever he caught a glimpse of the aged rat. But Splinter used all his ninja skills as he moved down the hill, and though one or two of the blasts left an aroma of scorched fur on the breeze, none of them wounded him. Ahead lay the perimeter fence. Splinter mustered his strength and jumped, clearing it in a gate vault. Back on the golf course, he felt more secure. He had spent the whole afternoon familiarizing himself with the terrain. Here he felt he had the advantage over his pursuer.

Upon reaching the wire, Karu cleared it in a single bound, as before. Native to a planet with much higher gravity than Earth's, he had no trouble with obstacles like that. But now he saw in annoyance that the Earth creature had somehow ducked out of sight. He drew out his infrared scanner and studied the ground through it. It displayed areas of coolness and warmth, showing his quarry's spoor as a series of fuzzy footprints across the grass. Tightening his grip on the ray gun, Karu set off in pursuit.

The trail brought him to the lake in the center of the course, then petered out at the water's edge. Karu clucked his tongue in admiration. The Earthling was smart, all right—but not smart enough. Karu started to follow the shore of the lake until he spotted a hollow reed poking up from the surface nearby. He adopted an expression that another Sirian would have recognized as a smile. Clever Earthling, using a reed as a snorkel. But not clever enough. Karu took aim at the reed and fired.

*Hisssss!* Instantly an immense cloud of steam formed where the laser beam hit the water. Karu scrambled back, startled. Only his fur saved him from being seriously scalded. Before he could recover his balance, a foot swept out from behind and knocked his gun into the lake.

Karu turned to face Splinter. "Eh?" He gasped into his translator. "But I thought . . ."

"What I wanted you to think, villain," said Splinter, lashing out with another kick. "Ninjitsu is the art of misdirection."

Karu backed off, blocking Splinter's attacks until he got the chance to press a stud on his harness. "What is the art of misdirection," he said with a sneer as he began to fade away, "compared to the science of invisibility?"

Within seconds he had vanished completely, screened by some sort of light-bending device built into his suit. It was a gadget that any ninja would have given his eyeteeth for, but Splinter had no time to dwell on that. Now he faced an invisible opponent and was unable to see to aim his blows—

—*Or parry,* he realized as a counter-attack from Karu sent him reeling. Obviously the alien was not averse to a bout of unarmed combat, as long as he had some way to gain an unfair advantage. Splinter slipped out of range and then turned as if to flee. *Of course, ninjitsu is among other things the art of the unfair advantage,* he reflected with a smile.

He could hear Karu behind him, bounding along in pursuit. The alien's long strides would soon allow him to outpace Splinter here on level ground. Fortunately, that was exactly what Splinter was counting on. He listened carefully, getting the rhythm of Karu's steps as he jogged nearer.

Suddenly Splinter turned and stopped dead, allowing Karu to catch up at last. "Here I am, Karu. Come and get me," he said, pretending to be out of breath. In fact he did not have to pretend very hard, as the physical activity at his age had proved quite tiring!

Karu, seeing his prey apparently exhausted, gave a guttural snarl of triumph and leapt straight at him. With perfect timing, Splinter ducked and the alien—unable to stop himself—went careening straight over his head. He landed smack in the middle of a sand trap.

It was the opportunity Splinter had planned for, and he was not going to waste it. The impact in the sand left him in no doubt where his invisible foe had landed. After snatching one of the flagposts to use as a bo, he rushed out across the sand and administered a mighty blow that sent sparks fizzing out of Karu's harness. The alien abruptly became visible again, the power supply to his suit's built-in devices disrupted by Splinter's strike.

Sprawled in the sand, it looked as if Karu were helpless. Splinter glanced back toward the woods. He was concerned for his pupils, and eager to get back and dig them out.

He should have known not to have taken his eyes off his enemy even for that split second. Karu drew a dart gun from his belt. Unlike his other paraphernalia, it worked on compressed air and did not use the suit's power supply. The dart it projected was tipped with a paralyzing nerve toxin. Now he had the meddlesome Earthling for sure. Splinter started to look back, but there was no time for him to take any evading action. . . .

Then suddenly something came whizzing through the air and smashed the dart gun out of Karu's hand. The object landed with a soft *plop* in the sand nearby, and both Karu and Splinter stared at it in amazement for an instant. It was a golf ball!

"Yoo-hoo! Master!" Michaelangelo called from the distance. "I think I'm getting the hang of this game."

"So—*FIZZ*—your companions dug themselves—*ZZAPT*—free," said Karu, his translator crackling with static because of the damage to his suit. He rose to a crouch in the sand and reached out toward the fallen dart gun.

"Excuse me," Splinter remarked ca-

sually, taking a step forward, "but are you aware that your tail is on fire?"

"What?" Karu asked in sudden horror, turning to look. He realized he had been tricked only when Splinter's makeshift bo swept his legs from under him and swung around to prod his throat before he could rise again.

"The oldest trick in the book," Splinter said as the Turtles came running up. "Those are the ones I like best."

"Master, you're okay!" said Michaelangelo, who was still holding the golf club he had used to make his shot at Karu. "We were worried."

"Not half as worried as I was, I'm sure, Michaelangelo. How did you get free so quickly, my sons?"

"Easy," said Leonardo, obviously very pleased with himself. "Instead of doing the obvious and tunneling *out,* we cleared the small amount of debris around the alien's ship. There were a few digging tools and things on board, of course. That's how he made the hidey hole for the ship in the first place."

"Excellent, my sons. You make me proud."

"What're we going to do with this bozo, though?" said Raphael. "A dude like him shouldn't be allowed to go free— but we can hardly turn him over to the law. They wouldn't believe in *us*, let alone an alien from Sirius."

"Yeah," said Donatello, "and *we're* the ones who look most like little green men."

Splinter narrowed his eyes and glared down at Karu. "You are disarmed and helpless now," he told the alien, "so I suggest you listen carefully."

"I shall," Karu replied dejectedly, his translator still struggling to keep up with his words. "You have—*FZZ*—bested me, and by the code of the—*FZZT*— hunt, I must abide by your terms."

"Very well. You will leave Earth and find some other planet for your sport. Moreover, you must pledge never to harm or kill another living thing for pleasure ever again."

Karu was mortified. "What is the point of—*FZZAT*—hunting if I cannot kill? Where is the—*ZZING*—sport in that?" He moaned.

"Hey, where's the 'sport' in shootin' at some dumb animal with a laser pistol, buster?" Raphael demanded.

"Thank *you*, Raphael," said Splinter, pretending to misunderstand, "but I don't quite count myself as a 'dumb animal.'" Turning back to Karu, he continued. "You may find that it is considerably more rewarding just to track the animals. Why kill them if you do not intend to eat them?"

"Yeah, take up photography if you have to shoot something!" said Donatello.

For all his protests, Karu's code of honor forced him to comply. He allowed them to lead him back to his spaceship, and within an hour he had blasted off from Earth, never to return.

"How are we going to explain this to Mieko?" Donatello wondered out loud.

"An alien hunter from another planet? She'll think we've gone crazy—it seems just too unbelievable!"

"If she was ready to accept a magical werefox," said Raphael, "then she ought to believe *anything*!"

As they watched the flare of the ship's rockets recede into the sky to be lost among the stars, Leonardo turned to have a private word with his venerable master. "You know, the duel between you two could easily have ended in tragedy," he said. "The alien was very skilled and—unlike you—he wouldn't have hesitated to kill. Foxes are notoriously cunning, after all."

"Maybe so, Leonardo," Splinter answered with a wink. "But rats are *sneaky*, and that wins every time."

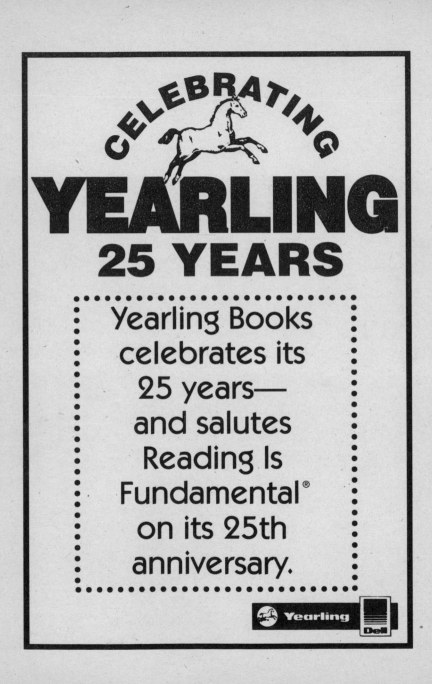

CELEBRATING

# YEARLING
## 25 YEARS

Yearling Books
celebrates its
25 years—
and salutes
Reading Is
Fundamental®
on its 25th
anniversary.

Yearling

Dell